PERILOUS CHANCE

PERILOUS CHANCE

❧

A tale of Auberon

by J.M. Ney-Grimm

Wild
Unicorn

ISBN-13: 978-0692022580
ISBN-10: 0692022589

Designed by JMNG

Cover art:

"Purple Lightning Bolt"
by Martine De Graaf / Dreamstime.com

"Griffon 01" by Henner Damke / Dreamstime.com

For all mothers and fathers
who have struggled with serious illness,
and for their families

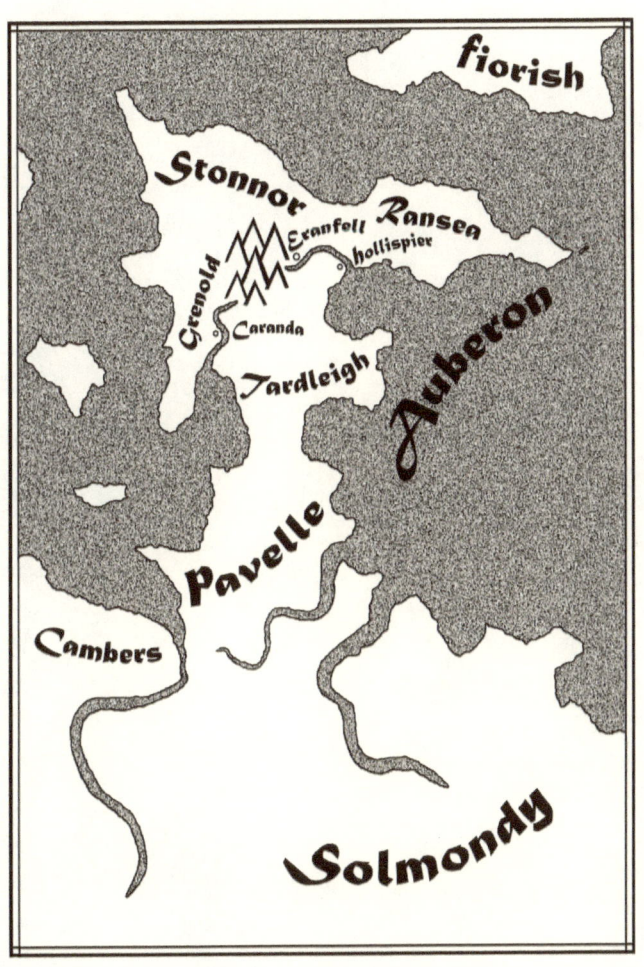

Clary and her sister Elspeth live in Ransea, the northeastern region of Auberon.

It's a rocky, bramble-grown penninsula with numerous quarries, as well as a cottage industry of preserve-making.

PERILOUS CHANCE

She was eleven, and she was hurt.

Her leg lay under her, knee throbbing. Her arm ached, the broken bone within sickening in its pain.

But worst of all, *worst* of all, a vast shadow loomed above her, dark wings spanning distances too great for the grotto enclosing them, razor-sharp talons sparking with the spitting blue fire of a strange power.

"No, please, no," she whispered.

How had it come to this? Her day had started so ordinarily, getting breakfast for herself and her sister, because Mama could not. She cast her thoughts desperately back to the morning.

I'm there. Not here. I'm there.

That morning, Clary had stood in the front room, turning slowly.

The cloth on the table under the windows hung askew, its corner tassel dragging on the weathered pine floor. The candles had guttered in their sockets, the wicks drowning amidst congealed wax. One, burned only halfway, lay fallen under the gluey drips from the gravy boat.

Clary's fingers crept to her mouth.

Why did this morning after an impromptu party feel so different?

The murmur of conversation last night, rising to her bed chamber, growing louder as the hour latened, had seemed normal. Uncle Maury's deep laugh boomed as always. Aunt Theosia's mandolin sounded as sweet.

But it hadn't been the same.

She stared at the welter of mismatched briar-wicker chairs, one tumbled on its side.

I won't think about that. Or who knocked it over.

But she knew who. *I won't think about it,* more fiercely.

Lyrus was whimpering upstairs in the nursery. She'd ignored him on her way down, hoping her mother would see to the baby. But she wouldn't. She hadn't risen before the children for . . . how long had it been? This was Thyril. Spring.

Had it truly been eight months? Last Sanember in fall?

Clary drew her fingers away from her lips to count, but she didn't really care how long it'd been. Too long. What she wanted to know was: would it end?

Mama hadn't been this bad all that time. But this last month. This last month with Papa being . . . *I won't think about it* . . . and Mama feeling his neglect. This spring had been bad.

Clary bit her lip.

A soft footfall sounded behind her. Then Elspeth crept to her side, slipping a small hand into hers. "Clary?" she whispered. "Lyrus's crying."

Clary knew. She could still hear him, faintly.

"There's some figs in syrup left over," she told her sister. No one had spilled wine in the dish, for a miracle. The bottles were empty, and the wine glasses held only dregs. "You could have them with some bread."

Elspeth shook her head. "Will you get it?"

Clary opened her mouth to say: get it yourself. But she didn't say it. *I'm the eldest. I'm stronger.* She didn't feel strong. Not right now.

The baby's wails were growing louder. She'd better not delay any longer.

"Okay."

Elspeth followed her back through the passage to the kitchen.

"You don't have to come," Clary urged.

Elspeth merely ducked her head and reached for Clary's hand again. Maybe she just wanted company?

The morning sun flooded through the kitchen's eastern windows, casting myriad small curls of shadow from the peeling white paint on the sills. Clary's grip on Elspeth's hand tightened. They navigated around the chopping table toward the vast range, avoiding the inner aisle between the table and the pantry cabinets.

Papa lay there on the bricks, quietened from his earlier snores.

Elspeth said nothing. Clary, nothing also.

The bread box on the counter under the windows proved empty. Clary sagged.

Elspeth darted to the canister at the counter's far end. "There's crisps!" She drew out a handful and handed two to her sister. Clary sighed.

It had been crisps yesterday. And the day before. She'd really hoped that today . . .

A resonant snore erupted from the uneven floor of the inner aisle.

Clary grabbed Elspeth's offering, clutched at her sister's other elbow, and fled.

Back in the front room, the baby's wails from upstairs acquired intermittent yells. Clary cleared a spot at the far end of the table, righted the chair, and settled Elspeth there.

She needs to sit. I'm not doing it because . . . I'm not *tidying. Not* – Clary shook head and grabbed a serving spoon. Her stomach rumbled, awake at last

The crisps were still crisp, not stale. If only she weren't so tired of them. The figs were sweet and chewy. Clary licked her thumb, sticky, then nibbled the last crumbs of cheese lingering on the cheese board. Elspeth raised the empty fig platter to her face, working on its gooey surface with her tongue.

Lyrus was shrieking now.

"Clary?" Their mother's washed-out voice drifted plaintively down the stairs at the other end of the room. "Can you see to the baby?"

"Yes, Mama," she called softly, tipping her chin up toward the ceiling. That *was* what came next. Was why she'd hurried her breakfast. Why did she delay now?

The sound of a groan from the kitchen – Papa – followed by a muffled thump, then the scrape of chair legs, urged her toward the nursery. Elspeth scurried on her heels.

Lyrus had pulled himself to standing by clutching his crib bars. His face, flushed red with crying, dripped tears. He held out his pudgy arms when Clary arrived in the doorway and plopped back on his bottom.

"Kah, kah," he whimpered.

She crossed to the crib, noticing the nursery was just as untidy as the front room below, and hoisted the baby up and over to her hip. Ugh! That nappy was beyond damp; more like sodden.

"Kah, kah." Lyrus buried his running nose in her neck. Mucous smeared wetly on her skin; tangled, blond curls tickled it.

Clary felt her own nose wrinkle, but only said, "Let's get you changed, Lye-lye."

Elspeth helped, chanting: "Ladybird, ladybird, fly away home, your house is aflood, and your children will drown," to distract the baby while Clary did the dirty work. The rhyme had several verses –house afire, children burn; house amire, children choke; and so on – but Lyrus seemed almost relieved to have his soiled nappy removed and didn't really require distraction.

"I could have done it," murmured Elspeth, rolling the dirty nappy into a closed ball and placing it in the overfull pail. Clary pulled a fresh baby dress from the cupboard with one hand, keeping the other firmly on Lyrus' belly. He was kicking energetically and demanding, "Nu nu! Nu nu!"

"It was my turn," insisted Elspeth.

Clary knew it. Why hadn't she let her younger sister see to Lyrus?

Half a year ago, she'd made a mess of nappy changing. But half a year ago, so had Clary. Now they were both neat and fast. They'd had to become so, when Mama just . . . stopped. Stopped cleaning, stopped cooking, stopped getting out of bed, stopped . . . caring? Not that she'd ever been very domestic. But some dusting and sweeping had happened. And she'd never neglected meals or preserve-making or Lyrus . . . or her daughters.

Clary dragged the baby dress – stained, but clean – over Lyrus' head, buttoned up the long back opening, and abandoned the struggle to jam his fat little feet into his shoes. At least his feet *were* fat.

I'm doing a good job. The way Mama would have wanted me to before . . . before.

Mama's room smelled of stale bed linens and dust. The drapes, dragged sloppily across the windows, created shafts of sunlight glaring through gloom. The shadows under the bed canopy shrouded Mama's stringy, unwashed hair and her creased pillowcase. When presented with her hungry infant, she shook her head and sighed wearily.

"I was awake with him all night. I can't."

Somehow, Clary didn't think so, but she gentled the protest creeping toward voice. Mama's cheeks *were* pale, her eyelids dark with fatigue. If she'd slept, it hadn't rested her.

"He needs to eat, Mama."

"I know." That note of tired impatience had once been a rarity. "Give him some goat's milk."

Clary looked at Elspeth.

Elspeth looked at Clary.

Papa was awake, and neither of them wanted to encounter him.

"Go on, then." Mama's sharp tone used to be reserved for evening bickering.

"Nu nu!" insisted Lyrus, but he clung to Clary. Clary hoisted him higher on her hip. Papa wouldn't be in the scullery where the milk cans stood. She might slip by the kitchen door unnoticed. If only Lyrus could keep quiet.

The baby chanted – nu-nu-nu-nu – all the way down the stairs.

"Ssh!" Clary whispered fiercely. "Ssh!"

Papa had opened the spigot to the cistern and was dunking his head in the sink. He didn't notice his children sneaking past the kitchen doorway. The running water gushed loudly, much louder than Lyrus.

In the scullery, Elspeth twisted the lid off the first milk canister: empty. The second held a thin skimming of liquid across its bottom. She turned dismayed eyes to her sister. "Oh, no! What'll we do?"

"Give it to him." The hard, grim sound to her own voice dismayed Clary more than the inadequate milk supply.

Collected from the wide canister into the narrow glass of a baby bottle, the milk made a better showing: it rose fully halfway toward the rubber nipple. Lyrus grabbed for the bottle eagerly, snatching it from Elspeth's hands. He'd likely finish in six gulping sucks. Clary turned toward the scullery door as grimly as she'd uttered her instruction to her little sister.

Their mother was not happy to see all three children back at her bedside.

"Can't you manage for five minutes without me?" she demanded. "Go ask your father, if you need something, and let me sleep."

Clary imagined herself simply dumping Lyrus down on the mattress and leaving. But the baby needed someone, if Mama refused him.

"He's still hungry," she stated.

Mama looked disconcerted. "He can't be."

"Aunt Mirren didn't bring the milk last night," Clary reminded her. "It's Lunday, not Wandy."

Mama sighed, and began opening the buttons of her nightgown. Lyrus went to her gladly. Over his curly head, Mama's face relaxed. She might not want to nurse her baby, but it did calm her. Her voice was kinder when she asked, "What are your plans for the morning, girls?"

"The cistern's full from all the spring rain." No working the pump till summer, likely. "Cousin Letty brought three baskets of clean clothes. Uncle Sorrelaude promised us a ham this evening. I opened a block of brunost cheese yesterday." Clary cataloged the household needs. "I thought I'd set Elspeth some spelling problems while I read history, but . . ." she faltered, then finished, "there's no bread."

Mama was nodding. "I'll bake bread later. There's a sponge ready in the pantry. But do your lessons after noon. The chervil conserve soured." Her mouth quirked. Something was wrong with the plants in their garden patch. "I want you to get me wild cabbage leaves from the old quarry instead."

Clary dipped her chin without protest and turned to go.

"No, stay." Did Mama sound apologetic? "I promised Dame Wicklander in the village . . ." Her voice trailed off.

"What did you promise?" Elspeth's voice reflected her eagerness for the errand. She liked Dame Wicklander.

Mama made a small noise of discontent. "That I'd bring her some of last year's bramble jelly. The baby dresses she's sewing for Lyrus are ready. But . . . you've missed too many lesson days already." Mama's regret became decision. "It can wait till tomorrow. I'll send word." Then she muttered, "I wish I could go myself."

Her mother's unexpected concern for her daughters melted Clary's resistance. And it would be a treat for Elspeth. "We'll go, Mama. There'll be time in the early evening for spelling and history."

Mama took some persuading, but the girls got their way and headed downstairs.

The garden trugs were stored under the counter in the kitchen, but Papa was gone. Was he even in the house? Clary wondered.

"Let's take some brunost cheese," Elspeth begged. "I didn't know we had any. And I'll get hungry before we come back."

Clary nodded. "And some dried bramble berries."

"Canteens?" added Elspeth.

"There's a spring."

"Oh. I forgot."

It didn't take long to assemble what they needed, plus the jelly jars for Dame Wicklander. Clary stepped out onto the kitchen stoop. The sunshine lay warm on her cheeks and forearms, but the chill of the old stone underfoot crept up through her boot soles. "We don't need our pelisses," she decided. "It will only get warmer, and the air lies still in the quarry."

They passed the herb garden and the berry patch on their way. None of the plants were leafing out properly, and the bramble canes featured an unnatural gray tinge to their brown bark skins. Clary shook her head. She had enough to worry about without that.

"What if Papa's at the quarry?" Elspeth voiced Clary's fear.

"He won't be. It's too early." Except today he was up earlier than normal.

"He goes there every day," persisted Elspeth. "To see that lady, I think. She's really pretty, isn't she?"

The woman spotted by the girls almost a month ago was more than pretty. Clary's memory flashed on the lovely line of her jaw, the fire in her dark eyes, her masses of dark curling hair. Who was she? They'd never seen her before, but she came every day to the quarry also.

Clary pushed down the resentment stirring inside her. Wild cabbage for Mama. Focus on that. If she got angry, then she'd have to notice why she was angry. And if she noticed why . . . everything would fall apart. *I'll just do the next thing.*

"If Papa's there, we'll hide," she told her sister.

"But how will we gather Mama's cabbage, if we're hiding?"

Clary repressed irritation. "We've always managed up to now." Papa *went* to the quarry. She knew he did. But they'd never actually met him there. "It'll be alright."

Elspeth brightened. "Maybe the lady will greet us. Maybe she's nice. Maybe she'll help Mama. She must live closer than Aunt Mirren and Aunt Theosia."

Clary shivered. "No. I think . . . we'd better hide from her also. If she's there."

They'd crouched down below the bramble stems the first time they saw her. The other times, she'd been leaving as they arrived, or they'd been leaving as she arrived. Had she even glimpsed them? Clary didn't think so. Too far.

Why don't I want her to see us?

Could she be a troll? Surely not. Trolls were old and ugly. And wicked.

But if she were a troll, she'd be dangerous. Trolls were patterners who got greedy and grabbed too much power in their magic patterning. It gave them troll-disease and made them crazy. If the stranger were a troll, maybe she'd ensorcelled Papa. Maybe that was why he roamed the bluffs instead of working in his studio on the marble horses for the fountain commissioned by the Morofane for the great square in the capital.

But she's beautiful. She can't be a troll.

In the abandoned quarry, it was late morning. Jennifry let her trug fall and stood as upright as she could get, rubbing the small of her back.

Oof, but bending hurt.

She surveyed her gatherings. A handful of wild asparagus, thin and new-sprouted. The last good leaves of winter's rampion. A salad's worth of fresh borage. And nettles, the leaves barely unfurled and soft.

That's enough.

She could return home, start blanching the nettles, preserving the rampion and borage conserve.

But the sun felt good on her cheeks. She lifted her face to the sky and closed her eyes. Warmth soaked into her brow, her throat, her shoulders. *Mmm.* Perhaps she could spare a few moments, linger longer in the sunshine, so grateful as the days grew longer.

But not visit the *orbis* – the *orbis* and its *energea*. That was better than sun, easing the deep ache in her bones and calming her thoughts. But something about it scared her. Could something that felt so good be bad?

She bent to lift her trug full of spring greens.

The laughter of little girls – familiar little girls – met her ears when she straightened.

They were gleaning above her, choosing leaves from the brink of the cliffs and joking.

"Clary, Clary, look! It's like green rabbit ears," trilled the younger one, flaxen curls jouncing under her mop cap.

"Like a doe with three kits," agreed her older sister, nodding and smiling.

Jennifry edged toward the cleft in the limestone behind her. She didn't want them to spot her.

She'd seen the girls often, of late, but always from concealment. Her stooped posture, large ears, and sagging eyelids would scare them. They'd think her a troll. And they'd be right about that; but wrong about the danger. She suffered troll-disease, but she'd never hurt them.

I won't go inside, all the way to the grotto. I'll just hide under that lip of rock at the entrance.

The brambles screening the crack scraped her cheek, drawing three drops of blood.

Jennifry sank to her knees and plucked a leaf of the comfrey growing there. Its sap would ease the scratch.

She could no longer see the girls – and doubted they could see her – but their voices rang clear.

"Not so near the edge, Elspeth," reprimanded the elder. "The rock gets crumbly, and the wild cabbage doesn't grow there anyway."

"Does too!" insisted Elspeth. "Look at that one."

"That's plantain," corrected her sister.

Comfrey pressed to her cheek, Jennifry felt the skin stretching as she smiled, her lips curving in memory.

We were about their age – maybe a year or two older – when we discovered the orbis. Kasharan was turned thirteen. I, almost twelve.

She pressed the herb leaf harder. Being eleven was a good memory. Finding the *orbis* in the grotto . . . more ambiguous. It was beautiful, the curving surface of it gleaming in swirls of cream and ivory, looming head height like the trap to their old ice-house.

Kasharan had stepped close to it, and her eyes lit with excitement. Her hand stretched as though she might grab the opalescent marvel – despite its massive size – and take it for all her own, but she started when her fingertips touched down.

"Oh!"

"Kasharan, what is it?" Jennifry had cried, anxious even then, before she knew what it was. Before she knew how grievously her sister could choose.

"It's good," Kasharan murmured, "really good." And closed her eyes.

I wanted to leave. It was too beautiful, too alluring. If only I had.

Instead she'd stood frozen, scared by the expression on her sister's face, but curious too, tempted.

"Mmm," breathed Kasharan. "Mmm."

And Jennifry stepped toward her, not away.

Closer, then closer still.

The *orbis* was slightly warm, and she felt peaceful. Her sister reached out one hand, circled Jennifry's wrist, and touched her palm to the lambent curve.

"Oh!" she cried, just like her sister.

She was peaceful no more, but she didn't pull away. This was dazzling, fizzy, fun. She was flying like a pegasus, soaring like a phoenix, climbing and diving like a star-drake. All while standing perfectly still. It *was* good, very good. And yet . . .

She wanted to pull away. And she didn't.

They'd returned home late in the gloaming and been scolded for it.

But Kasharan visited the *orbis* the next day and the next, dragging Jennifry with her, ignoring Jennifry's protests – *there's something wrong, something wrong* – and acting on Jennifry's unspoken consent: *yes.*

Was the *orbis* a troll's enchantment, that they made pilgrimage to it every morning for a sevenday?

The wild mix of elation and terror kept Jennifry silent. And compliant.

I should tell someone. I should do something. I should. But she'd said nothing, done nothing.

They went every day, then twice a day: straightaway at dawn, and once before bed.

"Jennifry, is it changing?" probed Kasharan. "I think it's different."

Jennifry hadn't thought so. It still felt good – very good. She didn't mind the startling fizziness so much anymore. Or the sudden internal swoops. And the warmth was just good. So good. Or had it gotten less fizzy? Less swoopy?

"I think it's changing," insisted Kasharan. "I don't want it to change."

That noon, Kasharan went to the miniature hot spring in the cleft, the nook where the *orbis* rested, to check on it.

"It's not as strong," she reported, worried. "Jennifry, what'll I do?"

Jennifry didn't know that answer, but she knew her sense of a problem growing larger was right.

Kasharan tried to drag her sister to the *orbis* the next noon, but Jennifry resisted. "It's not changing. We don't need to check it," she protested.

This time she didn't give in. There *was* something wrong, and even if she wouldn't tattle, neither would she concede.

But Kasharan checked. She got up from her bed in the wee hours of that night to visit their find.

Then at dawn, after breakfast, at noon, before supper, in the gloaming, by starlight.

Jennifry lost count of her sister's trips to the cleft in the old quarry.

And she covered for her. Gathering Kasharan's strewn clothes to the laundry basket. Sewing her sampler on the sly. Practicing her pieces on the harpsichord when Mama met with their housekeeper or cook – anything that drew her from the drawing room, so she didn't realize it was Jennifry playing Kasharan's music.

Kasharan showed no gratitude. "You should come with me," she scolded. "Help me save it!"

Jennifry winced.

"There's nothing wrong with the *orbis*, but there's something wrong with *you*," she dared.

Kasharan frowned, opened her lips to scold some more, then didn't. "Really?"

Jennifry nodded. "'Shara" – how to say it? she'd not said it to herself; just felt it – "you don't skip rope or roll hoops or read or ride Greylegs or . . . or . . . anything." How could she make Kasharan see what she saw? That all her sister's usual pursuits had just . . . stopped.

Kasharan was listening, a puzzled look on her face.

"You go to it too often!" Jennifry burst out.

"If I go less, will you come?"

Jennifry hesitated.

"If I go just . . . just three times, will you come?"

It had to be better, if she went less. Didn't it?

"*Please*, Jenny."

Jennifry sighed. Then acceded: "Alright."

The *orbis* seemed just as it had always been: glimmering softly amidst its mineral spring bath, soothingly warm, and thrillingly fizzy and swoopy. Touching it felt like coming home, and that scared Jennifry all over again.

"'Shara, I think three times is too many. Two times might be. Even *one*."

"Don't you dare go back on your promise, Jennifry nin Calcinides."

She hadn't promised; Kasharan had.

And Kasharan didn't stick by her promise.

They went four times that first day, then six, then nine. Jennifry didn't bother protesting. She'd lost. Not only to her sister, but to the *orbis*. Its halo of wonder proved too strong. *I need it now. Like Kasharan.*

Kasharan began formulating plans to "save" it using the patterning *energea* she was learning from Aunt Sophy. "I did sleep-and-heal yesterday, Jenny! I could heal the *orbis*! Keep it strong!"

Jennifry made different plans. In secret. She couldn't stop her sister. She couldn't stop *herself*. But she might just stop the *orbis*. I'm going to try, she vowed.

A sevenday later, they stood ankle-deep in the spring.

"I'll start first," instructed Kasharan.

Jennifry nodded. They'd been over the sequence a dozen times.

"Then you join me." Kasharan grabbed Jennifry's left hand. "You've been practicing, right? You remember what to do."

Jennifry nodded again. She'd been practicing sleep-and-heal, yes. She'd also been practicing something else. Something darker. Harder. Something listed in the back pages of Aunt Sophy's gramarye.

Kasharan closed her eyes, and Jennifry matched her breath to her sister's. Slowly in, slowly out. Soft and easy and free.

She opened her mind's eye. Silver filigree blinked into being, tracing the *energea* of her sister's arcs and radices, tracing her own: from sole to root, through belly and plexus and heart, out via throat and brow and crown and palm. *Ahh.* This was pattern making.

Cool blue trickled from Kasharan's fingers, flowing gently round the *orbis*, laving its surface with peace.

Be healed, be whole, be well.

"Now," whispered Kasharan. "Now."

Jennifry launched . . . her attack.

It was not gentle, was not blue, was not peaceful.

Black fire erupted from her palms, blasting Kasharan's healing gift aside, engulfing the *orbis* in thunderous violence.

Jennifry's silver lattice of radix-and-arc flashed searing gold, and she heard herself shrieking.

"Glory be horror, warmth grow chill, never thrill my spirit, bring splendor to *stop!*"

"Stop!" Kasharan's cry topped hers, and her sister's trickle of *energea* raged into torrent: fierce blue, fierce flood, fierce intent.

"No!" Kasharan's lattice flared gold, flared orange, glaring hot and parlous and corrosive. Her cataract of

azure turned cobalt, turned black, turned thunderous and vile as Jennifry's own.

This was not pattern making.

This was *incantatio* – bringer of troll-disease, herald of loss – the lurking danger awaiting a patterner who reached in power and greed.

Kasharan's blue-black tangled with Jennifry's ebon-black, sparking, spitting, backing up the orange conduits of the girls' arcs, drowning their radices in dark-burning fire.

The blazing inferno of eclipse intensified.

Winked out.

Jennifry found herself sitting waist-deep in water, tangled with her sprawled sister, who wept wrackingly.

Cradled within the *orbis* . . . a being awoke.

I am here.

He spun in liquid warmth, kicked out, and flipped over. He felt dizzy and happy. Here was nice, here was exciting, here was *here*!

A murmur sounded in the darkness, sweet and low.

Be thou whole, be thou one, be thou Ayr.

He was whole.

He was here.

He was *Ayr*.

Time passed in his warm lagoon, an interval of bliss and experiment. He reached and waved. He bent and swam. He swooped.

Be thou mine, be thou thine, be thou one.

I am thine.

I am mine.

I am *Ayr*.

Love lapped him and enfolded him. *Be thou strong, be thou winged, be thou fierce.*

I am strong. I am fierce. I am *Ayr!*

Ayr is winged, Ayr is crowned, Ayr is might.

I am flight, I am might, I am *Ayr!*

His mother's song swelled once more, celebrating him, then hushed and ceased.

She was gone!

She was gone, and he was ready.

I am here!

He stretched, he swooped, he strengthened. He grew. And grew.

Then another murmur.

Be healed, be whole, be well.

Mother? No, this voice sounded lighter, higher, and younger. Who?

Be healed, be whole, be well. Like Mother, she was *she*. Like Mother, she meant well, but her delight felt fizzier. She was . . . fledgling.

Sister! I am here!

They could fly together, swoop together, rule together!

He awaited her response. It came brutally: black, cold, and stinging. He choked. He flailed. He drowned.

No!

Stygian ice slammed him. He stilled. *Will I cease before I start?*

Another cold blow, so cold it burned. Burned and started a flame in his heart.

I am flight, I am might, I am Ayr! He was strong, he was mythic, he was stunning. *Sister-that-was, you shall not destroy me.*

He reached a different way, not with a limb, but with his awareness.

Where?

Where?

There!

There was power, there was force, there was *counter*.

He struck.

Silver fire erupted from his core, bursting outward, engulfing all, slapping aside the black cataract that devoured him.

Peace bloomed.

Ayr sighed. He was safe.

❧

*A*bove the quarry, Clary and Elspeth were drawing nearer along the cliff top. Jennifry could hear them, their innocent voices light on the sunlit air.

Below, within the shadowy cleft, Jennifry tensed and dropped the comfrey leaf. Once, she'd been young like they were. Now . . . it was well the rust-stained, creamy rock of the passage hid her.

She looked out through the sharp arch of its opening and across the quarry's sloping floor. Tough greens and messy brambles – edged by the sun's brightness – fountained from cracks between slabs of white limestone. The wildness drew her. But not so strongly as what she knew lay behind her in the grotto.

I'd better move, if I don't want them to see me when I leave.

She heaved to her feet. *Do they know they have a great aunt who's a troll?* She doubted it.

The Roanmothes hid madness in their lineage; likely the current rofane of the Calcinides hid the incantatrices in *his* descent. The old rofane – her father – had reached for secrecy fast enough. His discovery that his child harbored troll-disease still formed a bitter memory.

She and Kasharan had stumbled home in the dusk, dripping and disoriented, unaware of the fell change in the *energea* of their bodies.

Rofane Parthen and his wife were hosting a gala and never missed their daughters, who got themselves to bed unseen.

The morning revealed the truth. To them, if not to their mother and father.

Jennifry woke to Kasharan's shriek as she encountered her reflection in the dressing table mirror.

"What is it? What is it?" she'd gasped, tumbling from her curtained bedstead.

Her sister could not answer, but she didn't need to.

Two trolls stared out at them from the mirror's surface. Young ones, with firm rosy skin and bright eyes, but trolls.

Kasharan buried her face in her hands, while Jennifry stared.

Crow's feet framed those youthful eyes. That young nose took the shape of a crooked thumb. And plump handles of flesh curved the jawline on either side of that stubborn chin.

Hers.

Her eyes, her nose, her chin.

"Oh, no. Oh, no. Oh, no," she whispered.

Kasharan saved them.

Aunt Sophy's patterning lessons had reached *chimerae* and illusions, and Kasharan put her learning to work that dawn. When the sisters emerged from their bedchamber, all evidence of trollism lay hidden by a magical glamor, and Kasharan's deceptive skills grew strong with persistent use.

Jennifry's exposure came later.

Footfalls above her current hiding place pulled her back to the present.

Clary and Elspeth were too close for her to start home now without being seen. And she bore considerable risk by remaining barely under the cleft's entrance arch.

I'll take just a few steps inside, not more. Not enough to see, not far enough to touch – her thoughts veered away from her temptation.

This is far enough.

Within the dark warmth of the *orbis*, Ayr started from sleep.

Was he safe? Was it over?

He remembered a cold and cruel attack from a fledgling he'd called friend, and his own silver repulse.

What then? Had he died?

He stretched a tentative limb. Warmth and giving fluid swirled along his feathers.

I am live.

Relief flooded him, but with worry on its heels. What came next?

It might not be nice.

His first awareness of *being* had been nice. His mother's song had been nice. He'd thought all his sensations would be nice. But they hadn't.

Who had attacked him? And why?

He stretched another limb, and another.

Only warmth and more warmth and the liquid of his lagoon met his questing.

I am safe, he decided.

With safety came the impulse to move. He couldn't be still, but uncertainty curbed his exuberance.

I am hidden, I am shielded

Was he?

I am safe, he repeated, trying to shake his apprehension.

He worked his fore claws, kicked out with his hind paws, and mantled his wings. No hurt met his testing. *I am well.*

"Be thou whole, be thou well, be thou strong," spoke his memories. "Be thou puissant, be thou mighty, be thou strong."

I *am* strong.

And he was.

His limbs claimed vigor, and his confidence grew. *I am strong, I am well, I am Ayr!*

I am mighty.

I am fierce.

I am Ayr!

His dives grew daring; his swoops, more precipitate; and his somersaults, ebullient. Yet his joy carried fierceness in its wake. He'd recovered his courage, but not his innocence. Future friends would need to prove themselves.

⁃ 🐾 ⁃

Kasharan's magical glamor took on a life of its own. Not content with merely hiding the sisters' troll-disease, she made them beautiful.

Jennifry's flaxen curls acquired a silvery brightness, and her eyes deepened to the intense blue of the Sanember sky. The waif-like charm of her childhood became delicate loveliness as she approached womanhood. Kasharan's allure was bolder: brilliant black eyes, shining raven tresses, and a jawline where grace married strength.

Their suitors multiplied.

In time, Kasharan accepted one.

The son of Rofane Brusscente was clever, witty, and kind. If only he'd lived nearby, all could have been well.

When the carriage bearing Kasharan and her bridegroom to the Rivenpeaks crossed out of Ransea, her patterned glamor fell from Jennifry's troll-diseased body. She was short, not tall; dumpy, not slim; faded, not vibrant.

Her mother, the Rofanish, screamed.

The Rofane thundered: "What have you done to my daughter?" mistaking Jenny for a sudden-come stranger, and an enemy.

"Papa . . . it's me. Your Jenny. I'm . . . ill."

He'd understood then, all too quickly, and hustled her out of the ballroom where their guests waltzed and celebrated Kasharan's newly concluded nuptials.

In the deserted nursery – unoccupied by the handmaidens populating her bedchamber – he berated her. "How dare you steal power with *incantatio*! Were you jealous of her? Your sister? With her skill at patterning and her handsome husband?"

Jennifry shrank from him.

How could he think that? It was true she'd little gift for patterning, alas.

That first outpouring of illicit magic had been more illicit than she'd known: a perilous *incantatio* from the first flow of *energea* through her radices. And Aunt Sophy had never coaxed more than a trickle of the safe patterning from her since then. Especially because Jennifry had that dreadful black corrosive fire to conceal.

But she boasted as many suitors as her sister, and more offers of marriage. She'd dared accept none of them, given the hard truth of her disease. And her dependence on Kasharan's glamor.

Kasharan's choice to deceive her beloved had repulsed Jennifry. *How could she?* I couldn't bear doing that to . . . her thoughts shied away from his name.

With Jennifry's help, Kasharan had made many attempts to anchor her glamor in an item she could leave behind to protect her little sister. They'd tried Jenny's shoes, her prayer book, and even her own hair. Only the mirror in which they'd first witnessed their disease could hold the enchantment, and that apparently not in permanence.

The Rofane allowed Jennifry to pack her favorite gowns, her favorite books, and the trinkets from her dressing table. Its mirror still reflected her as beautiful,

although the glamor clung only to its surface and no longer around her person.

A two-wheeled hand cart piled with more practical necessities awaited her behind the carriage house. Her father's farewell was brusque and instructional: "Follow the path to old Tilde's hut. It's been cleaned for old Nurse, but I'll give her the cottage by the crossroads instead. I'll send Josef to you with more food in a sevenday."

Her mother neither bade her farewell nor witnessed her departure.

Darkness. Warmth. Safety.

The *orbis* provided all these.

Ayr's talons grew razor sharp, and his hind paws sported mighty claws.

But when the time came to shred the curving boundary of his fledgling world and emerge into a larger one, he could not. The shell resisted all his strength, all his passion, all his desire to be free. Slash of talon and buffet of paw availed nothing.

It would not crack.

Could not.

His wings outgrew the birth space first, curling down along the sphere, then under his legs and up the opposite arc. Within the carapace of his wings, his limbs lengthened and his torso gained bulk. Rigid limits cramped him, compressed him. The yolk sac supplying him with nourishment ran out. He grew hungry. Starving.

The attack in his infancy had become dim memory, but he hadn't forgotten it.

I survived its violence, but I may not survive this: its aftermath.

He felt certain his imprisonment possessed unnatural origins.

He delved deeper in memory, past the singing of his enemy into the songs of his mother, and then beyond those, beyond even the first simple awareness of *I am*. There in the darkness of non-being lay a portal into the heritage normally accessed after wings greeted air. He'd touched it unconsciously as a baby. Now he would do more than touch: he would claim it as his own.

He . . . *reached*. And surrounded and held.

This is mine.

Ribbons of silver sparkles streamed up his talons through his heart and into his great hooked beak. Jets of dazzling sapphire spurted into his hind claws and up his legs, through loins and belly and plexus.

This is *mine!*

He roared. He struck.

The shell of his prison did not break, but neither did it rebound the *energea* as it had his physical blows. His power passed out through the barrier, out through a passage, and sank deep into . . . richness, bounty, *sustenance*.

Here was food, here was healing, here was *life*.

He drew it into him to satiate his starvation, to soothe his aching limbs, to repair the damage of the old wrong dealt him by his enemy.

Some of the richness felt too new, too fresh. He learned to let it be.

Some of it felt old and fragile. He let that alone also.

And some of it was diseased. He avoided it.

But much more was scrumptious and sustaining. He fed.

His compression became density. *One day, I will emerge, and when I do my foe will know it.*

He consumed the life surrounding him, and the sapphire and silver *energea* of his heritage flowed all through his being. He lay still, poised for the moment when his density would overcome all. Poised in darkness, poised in ferocity, poised in crystallized wrath.

A whisper touched his hearing.

Be healed, be whole, be well.

His enemy!

But his density merely approached the needed threshold. He had not crossed over.

He hissed.

Very well. He would absorb this too. All bounty would be his. All *energea* would be his. All enmity would be his. He would be density upon density upon density.

He listened.

And learned it could not be his enemy. Sick, old, and frail, she was familiar, but not the same. And she meant him well. Or did she? He'd been mistaken before.

He listened.

Be healed, be whole, be well.

She visited him irregularly, but frequently, and always with a gift of *energea*.

She was friend, not foe.

Jennifry took two more steps along the rocky passage, and then another. Gentle ripples of light reflected by water moved over the textured limestone walls, brightening as she shuffled forward.

Did she wade through a stream, pulled by its current? No, the passage remained dry, as always. 'Twas her memories that drew her reluctant feet onward. Memory and longing, both stronger than willpower.

An eggy, mineral odor arrived on moisture-laden air.

She passed around the bend and stopped.

There it lay, bathed in warm aqua waters. Wreathed in steam. Vast and round and creamy white, whorled by cinnamon traceries. Casting a warm glow on the glistening limestone walls around it.

She stood just out of range for a touch, but mere proximity felt good.

Not as good as those early days, when the *orbis* was exciting, as well as comforting. But it soothed her aching bones and smoothed her worried thoughts.

Despite the edgy tautness underlying its peaceful warmth. *That* was more recently different. What did its tension mean?

She'd avoided the *orbis* for years after Kasharan departed Ransea, blaming it for her predicament.

Tilde's cottage was lonely and out-of-the-way.

Josef brought provisions and anything else she needed, but didn't stay to talk. Her father never came at all in those first few months and then sank to his deathbed before his rage could soften. Her mother risked the Rofane's displeasure with sneaking visits on the sly. These grew easier and more frequent after he died, then ceased altogether when she remarried and changed residences to live with her new husband.

Jennifry had a lot of time in which to think. And think she did, although not to good effect for some time.

She obsessed about her sister, torn between worry and resentment. She raged at her father: why had he condemned her, not helped her? She missed her mother – her namesake – even though the Rofanish Jennifry nish Calcinades had never been a terribly motherly sort. She wondered what explanation had been given to her brother, Arteme, away in the court of the Morofane.

Eventually her brooding grew as boring as it was uncomfortable.

Josef brought her an unrequested book on herb lore, and she read it. Learning about the plants in the weedy garden surrounding the cottage proved interesting, and she began taming the weeds. (Although some of them had unexpected uses – both culinary and medicinal.)

When she finished *Flora of Ransea*, she asked Josef to bring more like it.

She discovered she liked wild gleaning as well as domestic gardening, and conserving her harvest even more. She began sending samples of her thistle jelly or nettle ferment back with Josef when he brought her word of a sick child or injured granny. She wondered what he told the recipients of her gifts, but didn't ask.

As her knowledge deepened, the books she wanted grew more esoteric. Volumes of philosophy and treatises on the marriage of mind and body hinted at other dimensions to physical healing. And reminded her of past choices. She'd let go of her sister's wrong, her father's, even her mother's. (How could a mother abandon her child? Even a child grown to womanhood and defiled by troll-disease?) But what about her own wrongs?

I stayed silent, when I should have spoken.

I said yes, when I should have said no.

And I lashed out, once all power to say no was gone.

It was that last deed that troubled her now.

She'd been a child for all three mistakes, but that didn't lessen their dire results. Her silence had led to her that "yes," which led to her violent action. The first two wrongs were truly wrong only in that they led to the last. But that last . . . her sister was a troll because of it.

(So was she, herself. Did she owe herself amends?)

And what of the *orbis*? Surely it was something live?

A dragon's egg? Or did pegasi hatch? She didn't know.

But if it were live, it must have taken some hurt.

She wished she could go back now and do things differently. But she couldn't. If she owed herself atonement, she didn't know how to make it. And her sister had forged her own solution. But the *orbis* . . . might await her succor.

I owe *it*, she decided. And visited its womb-cleft.

It seemed unharmed. But her experience of its aura *was* different: calmer, less frenetic. Was the change in her? Or in it? Was it the effect of time passing? Or the lingering aftermath of her *incantatio*? *It doesn't matter. I choose to give.*

Be healed, be whole, be well.

She'd visited it ever since, feeding it the small *energea* she'd learned under Aunt Sophy, guarding against the dangerous troll-magic that had overtaken her when she outstretched her patterning limits.

Be healed, be whole, be well.

For years she'd wished it well and given it healing. Could that make up for her attack?

I don't think so, but this isn't about righting wrongs.
Some wrongs couldn't be fixed. This was about doing
the right thing now. *I can't change the past. I can only act
now.*

So she'd acted, as best she knew how.

The energy of the *orbis* had changed again last
autumn, becoming imbued with a sense of fateful
waiting. Readiness.

For what did it wait?

And now it was different again: tense, expectant,
fierce.

Crack!

Jennifry stiffened. *Holy Teyo!*

More startling than the sound was the abrupt end
of the warm peacefulness normal to this spot. She felt
desperate, urgent, and hungry. Or, rather, she felt the
desperation and urgency and hunger radiating from
the *egg*.

It *was* an egg, she realized, an egg on the verge of
hatching, with a hatchling poised to gobble the nearest
morsel of warmblooded food available.

She fled.

How far away was far enough? How far away was
safe? The rock walls of the twisting passage streamed

by, then the shadow of the entrance arch, and Jennifry passed into sunlight.

A scream split the air.

Jennifry spun in time to see the littlest girl pitch over the brink of the cliff, dragging her sister with her when Clary refused to let go her frantic grab for Elspeth's arm.

Jennifry jerked herself back toward them – toward the bluff – fast enough to wrench her wrist when her hand tangled in Elspeth's petticoats.

Not fast enough to break the girls' tumbling fall.

The muffled thud of slight bodies on packed earth seemed almost innocuous.

The faint crack of bone – as the elder sister, slightly above the younger in their descent, landed – sounded equally meager.

How could misfortune arrive with so little fanfare? Jennifry's thoughts touched her own past disaster, more flashy, but similarly opaque upon arrival in its true meaning.

The girls' greenish white faces, shocked and afraid, told a realer truth.

Clary reared to her knees, arms rising before her face, prepared to defend her sister even now, breathless from her plummet.

❧

One moment they stood amidst thin sunlight, cool airs stirring about them while they picked wild greens at the edge of the quarry cliff. The next: a glimpse of the troll's slumped face and startled glance, Clary's wild grab for her sister's arm, the slide of gravel and dust beneath their shoe soles, and the abrupt plunge into the quarry.

Clary surged to her feet, hands rising to block . . . whatever came, the left arm throbbing with a sickening ache.

You won't hurt my sister. I'll hurt you first.

The troll stopped, drooping eyes . . . appalled? How could it be appalled? *It* was the appalling one.

"Don't you dare!" gasped Clary.

The troll shook its – her? it *was* wearing a dress – head.

"Please . . . I think your arm is broken." The voice, unexpectedly clear and pleasant, held pleading in its tones. "Let me help you."

Clary felt her own eyes widening. This was not how a troll should behave. Trolls were wicked and greedy. They helped no one save themselves. Everyone knew that. Was this some trick? She peered around her raised forearms.

Wrinkles framed the troll's eyes, folds of flesh rumpled its cheeks and neck, globules of fat hung from either side of its jaw. It was a troll, no question, for all that its skin flushed rosier than the pictures in Aunt Genevieve's catechism.

"Why?" Clary asked.

"And I think your sister's leg is broken. Please." The troll cradled its own arm. Had it – she – tried to soften their landing? "I won't harm you. I just want to help."

She didn't approach, waiting on Clary's permission.

Clary could hear Elspeth moaning behind her.

"What will you do?"

The troll's face softened. "I can't do much right away. I need the splints and bandages from my cottage, but I have some little skill with minor patterning. A trickle of healing *energea* right now will ease the pain and lessen the damage."

Clary stared. "Trolls don't use *energea*. You're an incantatrice, not a patterner," she accused.

The troll shook her head. "Only once, only by accident."

Clary considered.

Elspeth whimpered.

Clary nodded.

The troll wasted no time, kneeling, tracing Elspeth's pattern of radices and arcs, then closing her eyes and . . . concentrating.

Elspeth sighed and spoke in a thready tone, "Oh, Clary, it's better. Let her do your arm."

Clary did let her, and it did help. But her suspicion stayed strong.

"Why are you nice? Why are you helping us? Who *are* you?"

The troll got her knees under her, preparing to rise. "Let me go get my medicines and bandaging. You could walk home without further hurt to your arm, but Elspeth shouldn't be moved until her leg is splinted."

Clary's suspicion hardened. "How do you know Elspeth's name?"

"I heard you talking." The troll's reply was mild.

Clary could tell she was telling the truth. She could also tell there was more to it than that. Her lips compressed and her chin jutted, but her challenge remained unspoken.

The troll sighed. "I'm Jennifry nin Calcinides."

"You're not my great gran!" exclaimed Clary. "She died before I was born!"

This time the troll stayed silent.

"Oh, nin. Not nish." Clary blushed. Nish meant 'wife of the rofane.' Nin meant 'child of.' "Mama's aunt? Great gran's daughter?"

Jennifry nodded. "Will you stay here? Wait for me?"

"I never knew Great Uncle Arteme had a sister," Clary marveled.

Jennifry's smile was sad. "Don't move, alright? Especially don't move Elspeth. Or let her move herself." She hesitated, then continued, "It will take me at least half a glass to walk to my cottage and back. It will likely seem long, but please don't try to get home by yourselves."

Clary nodded, and Jennifry left.

She wasn't fast.

The sun moved past the cliff's brink, casting a sliver of new shadow before she reached the top of the path – winding up the quarry side to the rough, brambly land above it – and passed out of sight.

Clary looked at Elspeth. Her pinafore was rumpled and ripped; her dress beneath it, dusty; and her black wool stockings, loose from their moorings. But slight color had returned to her face, and she lay easily, a look of introspection upon her. "What other secrets are there, do you think?" she asked.

Clary shook her head. "Gran said Great Granfer Maxim – Rofane Roanmothe – had a brother who thought he was a wolf. But . . ." Her thoughts drifted to her nearer family. Would Papa's drunkenness of this last month become a secret? Mama's refusal to leave her bed?

Clary looked down at her own broken limb. Its sharp pain had ebbed and the throbbing lessened, but how could she manage Lyrus with a splint and a sling? How could Elspeth help, when she'd surely be on crutches?

I can't do anything about that right now.

The sun edged farther west, and the bluff's shadow crept out to shade Elspeth's eyes. How much longer would it be?

The breeze rustled the brambles above.

A lark trilled, briefly.

Footsteps sounded.

Jennifry? Great Aunt Jennifry, Clary corrected herself, craning her head to spot whoever approached. The steps were too quick to be her great aunt's. Papa?

No, not anyone familiar, but Clary had seen this woman before: the dark beauty with that hint of cruelty to her expression.

She was beautiful yet. And her mouth still curved triumphantly. But something was different.

Clary squinted, blinked. What was she seeing?

A blur? A flicker? A wink?

A . . . troll?

Holy Teyo, no! If this woman were a troll, she was not benign.

Clary scrambled to her feet, scurried around Elspeth, and – using her good arm – grabbed her sister's shoulder, twisted her fingers in the fabric of pinafore and dress, and pulled.

"Clary, what are you doing?!" Elspeth's question was a frightened whisper, thank Teyo.

"She's dangerous. We have to hide."

Had Elspeth seen the woman? The troll? (Clary was sure the intruder was a troll. Even though she was beautiful.) Would her sister argue? Resist?

Clary pulled. Dragged Elspeth closer to the cliff face, into the shallow cleft waiting there, then around a bend into a hidden passage. Had it been here this whole time? How had she and Elspeth never discovered it before? The quarry was their play ground as much as their gleaning spot.

"This is far enough," gasped Elspeth. How badly had the dragging jostled her leg?

"No. It isn't," insisted Clary. "What if she comes after us?"

"Did she see us? I don't think she saw us."

Clary kept pulling, backing farther into the cleft. Where was the light coming from? Sunshine reflecting on the limestone near the entrance shouldn't be making it around that bend. She glanced over her shoulder. Oh!

Looming head high, the massive orb of creamy rock gleamed, casting its soft glow on the water swirling through the puddle in which it rested, and along the stalactites and stalagmites fringing the small grotto.

"What is it?" whispered Elspeth.

Clary became aware that she'd frozen in place. "I don't know. It looks like a giant goose egg made of agate, but . . ."

"What?"

Elspeth faced the way they'd come. She couldn't see it. Clary shifted her sideways, which was a mistake.

"Ow! Don't," whimpered her sister.

Clary looked around for something to prop Elspeth's shoulders – nothing – then lowered herself gingerly to make her lap into a pillow for Elspeth's head. She jostled her own arm, but managed to swallow her exclamation of pain.

Elspeth's eyes were screwed shut. "Ow, ow, ow," she moaned.

Clary scrutinized her sister's leg. Dare she move it? The sideways movement had bent it ever so slightly. Surely it needed to be straight.

"Elspeth, I have to move your leg."

Elspeth's eyes flew open. "Oh, don't! Don't!" Her voice was frantic.

Clary hesitated. Getting out from under Elspeth and then back to her feet seemed daunting.

"Clary, it hurts! It hurts so much!"

Teyo! She *had* to do something.

Awkwardly, she got her feet under her, holding her broken arm still, gripping Elspeth's pinafore at the shoulder with the other hand. She pushed upward with her legs, hitching Elspeth along the grotto floor (and straightening that leg), then losing her own balance. "Ack!"

"Ow!" cried Elspeth.

"Ow!" echoed Clary, as she fell against the glowing orb.

Its curving rock caught her, but the impact jolted her arm. She slid down the slick surface, landing half-in and half-out of the water, Elspeth's head miraculously back on her lap, not dropped on hard floor or underwater. She relaxed her grip of pinafore and lowered her voice. Their cries hadn't been soft. "Are you alright?"

The water was warm, as was the stone of the orb. She felt it vibrating against her ribs and upper arm – the good arm.

"You were right," panted Elspeth, her face pale

and clammy. "It's better this way, but –" She shook her head. And noticed the orb. "Oh! That's what you saw."

"I think it's alive."

Elspeth reached a tentative hand toward an ivory and cream swirl. "It's warm," she whispered. "It feels . . . dangerous. And . . . hungry!" She snatched her hand back, then reached out again.

Clary nodded. "I think it's an egg. Getting ready to hatch. Hatchlings are hungry, aren't they?"

"Clary, I don't want to be food," quavered Elspeth.

"Oh!" It hadn't occurred to her that she might be a meal to a roc or a hippogriff. "Maybe it's a pegasus egg. Pegasi are good, aren't they?"

"I don't think they're born from eggs," Elspeth faltered.

"They have wings though," urged Clary.

Firm footsteps slapped the passage floor, and the beautiful troll – Clary still thought she was a troll – rounded the bend.

They *hadn't* gone far enough.

Clary raised her broken arm, inadequate shield though it was, but the woman – the troll – ignored her.

"I knew it! Jenny never could get scrying right!" The troll's voice was edged, but refined. "And now I'm late. Likely too late!"

She strode directly to the egg, her toes stopping a finger's width from Elspeth's hip, the lace of her petticoat foaming over Elspeth's pinafore. She placed her palms against the egg's surface, and Clary felt the vibration against her ribs change: tighter, faster, urgent.

I am fit, I am full, I am Ayr! sounded in Clary's mind.

Crack! The egg rocked.

And rocked again.

The troll stiffened. Small crackles of orange lightning haloed her dress sleeves.

I am air, I am I, I am Ayr!

"I am witch, I am sybil, I am troll!" the witch declaimed.

Clary hunched away from her. *I knew she was a troll. Crack!*

I am here, I arrive, I am here!

"Never here, only there, stay within!" Stridency limned the witch's voice.

"Elspeth, she's trying to keep it from being born!" Clary murmured.

"That's good! It can't eat us, if it stays in its egg!" Elspeth whispered back.

"It's not right. And *she's* not good. It can't be good, if she's doing it. We should stop her."

"How?" Was Elspeth agreeing?

"Can you grip her ankles when I jump up?"

Elspeth nodded. "Hurry! It's getting worse. Can you feel it?"

Clary could.

The egg buzzed and juddered. The orange sparks racing down the troll's arms turned black. The water soaking Clary's skirts chilled.

No! Eggs needed warmth!

She felt Elspeth lean forward and grab.

She sprang up, butting her head into the troll's belly.

She felt herself falling, feet tangled in her sister's pinafore, neck clamped under the witch's strangling elbow.

The grotto floor was hard, and her broken arm twisted under her weight.

She screamed, heard Elspeth screaming. What had the witch done to her sister's leg?

She shoved at the weight pinning her down, never mind the sickening wrench to her arm, and rolled over when the witch released her.

"Little brats!"

The witch slapped her face, bouncing Clary's head with the force of the blow.

Then she was up, ignoring Clary, and kicking the welter of Elspeth's petticoat free of her pointed shoes, returning her attention to the egg, but no longer unopposed.

Jennifry had returned.

"Kasharan. No."

Clary could see she was outraged, despite the evenness of her words.

"What have you done?" Jennifry's voice quavered.

"What you should have done long since, sister mine." *Sister? Was she another secret great aunt?* "How could you think we had months yet? How could I have been fool enough to trust you?" Was that anguish in the witch's voice? "This is why I came home! I *need* this." Her arm came up, and she *threw* dark lightning – not at the egg – but at Jennifry.

Jennifry screamed and went down.

Crack!

The egg split in two and dimmed, darkening the grotto.

Looming shadow, sleek and lithe and fierce, leaped from the shell, talons stretched, razor beak agape.

Snick! Snap!

The witch was gone, swallowed down that hungry gullet.

❧

Swallowing richness, swallowing his friend's *energea*, achieving density, Ayr strengthened. Soon he would be ready. Soon he would triumph. Soon he would emerge.

Ayr fed.

And woke in time to know his birth crisis had come.

Now!

He could not buffet or rap or strike. His quarters held him too close for that. But he was strong, and great, and ready.

He pushed.

Crack!

He felt the shell of his prison quiver. He pushed again, talons and paws pressed against one curving limit, back and wing humeri crushed against its opposite.

Crack!

His prison swayed.

He reached for the source of his own *energea* and felt it flood his sinews. Blue lightning crackled through his bones.

I am fit, I am full, I am Ayr!

Then an orange lightning from without answered him.

"I am witch, I am sybil, I am troll!" declaimed his foe.

My enemy! This time he knew how to dominate her evil. He . . . swallowed and grew greater.

Crack!

I arrive, I am here, I arrive!

The orange lightnings grew black and hurt him. He swallowed.

"Never here, only there, stay within!"

Ayr felt his limbs chilling, his strength ebbing. *No!*

Then came unexpected respite, a moment of peace. He *heaved*.

Crack!

The limits compressing him fell away, releasing his cramped limbs to freedom, exquisite in its sensation. He stretched: forelegs and talons extended, hind legs and paws surging, wings sweeping, great rostrum gaping.

He leaped.

And saw his enemy confront his friend. *No!*

Snick! Snap! His foe was food. Succulent and savory and moist. A food wholly different from the intangible *energea* he'd consumed for so long. Food! He wanted more and looked for it.

He found something else.

The damaged body of his friend met his searching gaze. She and her . . . hatchlings? They were small, and they were hers. He could see that. And they were broken. He was too late.

His enemy was their enemy, and she had struck before his release.

No!

He reached again for his ancestral power.

Upon Jennifry's return to the quarry, the sun had shone lower in the sky. The light held a deeper golden tone, and a mild breeze fluttered the scruffy weeds fringing this craggy cup in the land. The smell of warm rock dust mingled with the sharpness of wild onion. Her knees hurt. She'd hurried.

But girls were gone, and somehow Jennifry knew they'd not headed home.

"Oh, no. Oh, no," she muttered. "They've gone inside, they've found it."

Would this be a second set of sisters lost to the *orbis* and troll-disease?

She hastened her steps as she followed the narrow track winding down the bluff. *I must save them.*

The shadow before the cleft entrance felt cool.

Crack!

The passage resounded with a blow, a violence, a birth.

Holy Teyo! It's hatching.

Twin screams echoed one after another, and she emerged into the grotto as Kasharan growled, "Little brats!" and slapped Clary's head against the stone floor.

"Kasharan. No."

She felt a fury ignite within her, like nothing she'd ever known before. What had her sister done to these nieces of theirs? How could she? How dared she?

Jennifry missed her sister's reply, starting forward in urgency.

Kasharan's attack did not miss.

Black lightning took Jenny full in the stomach like a whip from hell.

She fell, curling around her wound.

Clary lay still while the vast shadow of the creature loomed above her, mantling its wings, filling the grotto's space.

Her leg bent beneath her, its knee twisted.

Her arm throbbed at her side.

Her voice whispered: "No, please, no."

I am here, I am Ayr, I am strong, thundered the creature in her mind.

I am mighty, I am puissant! It paused. *Gryphon regnant am I!*

Blue sparks chased down its talons and leaped to her belly.

"No!" she cried out. But it felt good. Cool relief flowed through her limbs, banishing hurt, banishing pain.

The gryphon sprang away from her to bless Elspeth, and then away from Elspeth to Jennifry.

Be thou healed, be thou whole, be thou thine.

Then it was gone, hurtling through the passage, seeking the heavens that would be its home.

Clary wished she could see it as it mounted to the air: plumage gleaming in the sun, its fierce eye dominating all, its tremendous wingspan claiming sky.

I'm glad it's born. I'm glad it's free. I'm glad I saw it.

The broken halves of the egg shell lit again, the glow illuminating the grotto again.

She pushed herself up to sitting and saw her sister doing likewise. Had the gryphon's gift healed her leg? Apparently so. They crept to Jennifry's side.

Clary gasped.

Jennifry's eyes were open, but she lay as one stunned. Or dead. And the clear gray of her eyes remained the only thing recognizable about her.

Where was her wound? Where was her age? Where was her *troll-disease*? Was this really Jennifry?

Clary shrank from her.

Were all bad things made good? How could rightness feel so wrong?

Elspeth whimpered. "Clary, I'm scared."

Clary buried her face in Elspeth's shoulder, felt Elspeth bury her own in Clary's.

"I'm scared, too," whispered Clary.

"Pull me to its shell." Jennifry's murmur came low and sweet. "Please."

Clary whipped her head around, startled. *Was* it Jennifry?

"The birth liquors will ease me," Jennifry entreated them.

Slowly, Clary nodded.

"Can you do it?" she asked her sister. "Is your leg . . . ?"

Elspeth smiled tremulously. "I'm well, Clary. As though I never fell."

They turned to their great aunt.

Why wasn't she well? Or . . . why was she healed, but somehow not?

Jennifry opened her hands, pleading.

I guess my questions must wait.

Clary bent to take her great aunt's shoulders, Elspeth right beside her, Elspeth's hands right beside Clary's, gripping the loose fabric of Jennifry's now ill-fitting gown as they dragged her across the grotto floor.

The nearer fragment of egg shell – the larger – lay clear of the mineral spring and tipped. Silver-whorled fluid puddled within it and around it.

Jennifry sighed as egg's curve cradled her. "Ah. Thank you."

Clary opened her lips to speak, then closed them.

She looked at Elspeth.

Elspeth looked at her.

As one, they bent to the birth waters of the gryphon and began to anoint Jennifry's face and hands with the moisture.

Later, much later, Clary voiced her questions.

"The gryphon anchored my radices," Jennifry told her. "You do know that's what makes a troll, don't you? When a pattern-maker draws too much *energea* through the anchor points of her own pattern, they break and she becomes a troll."

Yes, Clary knew that. Every child learned it in lessons right along with geography and history and spelling.

"I thought it couldn't be cured." There lay her true objection. "But you are cured, right? You're not a troll anymore, are you?"

"No, I'm not." Jennifry shook her head. "It feels very odd."

"But . . ."

"I know. But!" She climbed to her feet.

Clary stared at her.

Her great aunt was still short, but her once-dumpy figure was now slight and graceful under the slack folds of her clothes. Her face was young and pretty and held a dash of pixie mischief in the eyes.

"Our world is upside down." Jennifry took Elspeth's hand on one side and Clary's on the other, drawing them gently toward the outside. "A gryphon is a game changer," she continued. "It makes the rules. I suppose it can change them. But it's not a comfortable thing, is it?"

Clary clutched Jennifry's hand harder. That was it. It was scary when an impossibility became a reality. Even when the new reality was good.

"Will it come back?" Elspeth whispered.

Jennifry didn't answer for a few steps.

Would it come back? Clary half-longed for it to return, half-feared it.

What else might it change?

"No," Jennifry decided at last. "The world would break, if it suffered many gifts such as this one. I don't think a gryphon can alight without giving. And yet our world hasn't broken."

"They must not visit us often," Clary mused.

"Good!" breathed Elspeth.

It was early evening when they got home, but the sun lingered some way above the horizon, golden in a deep turquoise sky, prelude to the splash of peach and lavender that would herald its setting. A swift darted over the highest boughs of the oak in the front garden, and Clary's heart skipped a beat, fear and longing co-mingled again. No, it was bird, not gryphon.

She sighed.

The front door stood open. Elspeth darted forward, then stood astonished on the threshold. What? Clary quickened her stride, outdistancing Jennifry behind her. Had something else gone wrong while they'd been gone? Maybe the gryphon's passage had disrupted things here as much as it had in the old quarry.

Good heavens!

Clary stopped beside her sister, feet glued to the spot.

The front parlor spread tidily before her: furniture upright, hangings straight, table cleared, and Papa lifting a last chair into place while Mama swept crumbs into a dustpan. Then Mama caught sight of her daughters, and the broom slipped – *clack* – to the floorboards.

She ran to them, crying, "Tiber, Tiber, they're here!" and caught them in her arms, her face wet with tears.

Papa rushed forward an instant later, encompassing all three of them in a wild embrace, but his voice whispered – reverence gilding gratitude – "Thank god, thank God."

Their tumble of joy and thanksgiving delayed explanations for a while. And the explanations, when they came, started incoherently – from both sides.

Eventually Jennifry, hovering in the doorway until then, entered the conversation: the egg, her sister, the gryphon, the world upside down.

The tumult after that bore a more purposeful character: young Pomfrey from the cottage down the lane sent for the job carriage, Lyrus fetched from his nap, Jennifry lent clothes for their visit to the Justicar of the Peace, and the carriage ride to his manor.

And then yet more bustle.

Rofane ni Calcinides seemed just as bewildered by their account of the events at the old quarry as Mama and Papa had been. He was *more* bewildered by the sudden appearance of his aunt, magically healed and young. Despite his confusion, once he acquired the gist, he acted with dispatch. He summoned the wardens under his authority, instructed his housekeeper to make a room ready for Jennifry, consigned Clary's family to his wife's care, and set off for the quarry to investigate.

The Rofanish fed them dinner and entertained them in her parlor after it. The stars pricked out in the darkening sky outside. When the Rofane continued absent, the Rofanish served tea and pressed them to accept beds for the night.

Mama declined. "We'd really rather return home, if we may. Will Ni Calcinides . . . ?"

"Oh, heavens!" His rofanish was impatient. "It's not as though Arteme doesn't know where you live! He can ride over when he has more questions."

And so they'd come home.

Mama changed Lyrus' nappy – he didn't wake, worn out – and laid him in his crib, asleep. Mama and Papa together put the girls to bed, Mama singing lullabies, Papa stroking Elspeth's hair. It was almost as though they'd returned from a year's sea voyage and couldn't bear to be parted from their children for any reason.

Once Clary had brushed her teeth, Mama invited her into the dressing room to braid Clary's hair. She was very gentle with the tangles, and then drew her daughter onto her lap in the rocking chair after the braiding was done. Her body felt solid behind Clary's shoulders and her arms like a soft quilt on a stormy night, although this night was still.

"I'm so sorry," murmured Mama, her fingers warm on Clary's cheek. "So very sorry. I can't imagine what this year has been for you. Other than awful."

"Mmm." Clary snuggled deeper into Mama's embrace.

Papa seated himself on the footstool at Mama's knee, rested his hand on Clary's hand.

"This year will be different." Clary could hear the promise in his voice."

Mama sighed. "It can't make up for . . . all the neglect."

"No." Papa pressed Clary's fingers. "But it can heal. Will heal."

The blue sparkles of the gryphon's gift arose in Clary's memory. "I'm already healed," she murmured.

"It might take you longer to trust us again," suggested Papa.

"Maybe."

But Clary didn't think so. Her parents were back.

Not from sea, but from long illness, the long draining of the gryphon's delayed birth. She knew they would not be going away again. And yet . . .

"Papa?" She heard her tone sharpen. "Why did you visit the old quarry every day?" *Had* he been visiting Kasharan? Betraying Mama?

His mouth straightened. "I never made it that far. I could feel that the wrongness, the weight on my limbs, came from that direction. But it grew heavier so rapidly that I sank to the ground before I got halfway. I had to crawl home when I came out of my faint." He shook his head. "Each day I swore I'd make it. *This* time. Find the source, find it and fix it. But I never did." His hand patted Clary's shoulder. "Like your mama, I'm sorry too. Sorry I failed you. Failed all of you." He paused. "A papa likes to protect his family himself. Not leave it to his children."

"We did help," murmured Clary, "at least a little."

Papa chuckled, leaving his grimness for the moment. "A little?" he repeated. "No, you and Elspeth were the nail that secured the horseshoe that steadied the steed that bore the knight who saved the battle. Sometimes the littlest things are the biggest."

Clary smiled. Papa was here. Mama was here. She was home.

THE END

APPENDICES

Clary's Home

Clary lives in a comfortable cottage with half-timbered walls and a thatched roof.

Her father's studio, where he sculpts stone into marvelous stauary, occupies a separate outbuilding. He keeps the accounts for his commissions in the library of the cottage.

Clary's mother's "sewing room" sees more of Clary's and Elspeth's school lessons, cozy mother-daughter chats, and late family suppers than it does stitchery.

Clary and Elspeth share a bedchamber.

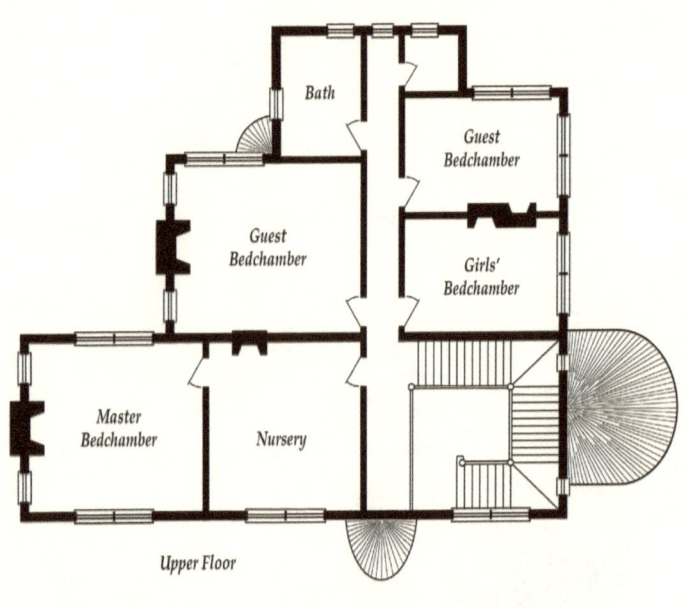

Bath

Guest
Bedchamber

Guest
Bedchamber

Girls'
Bedchamber

Master
Bedchamber

Nursery

Upper Floor

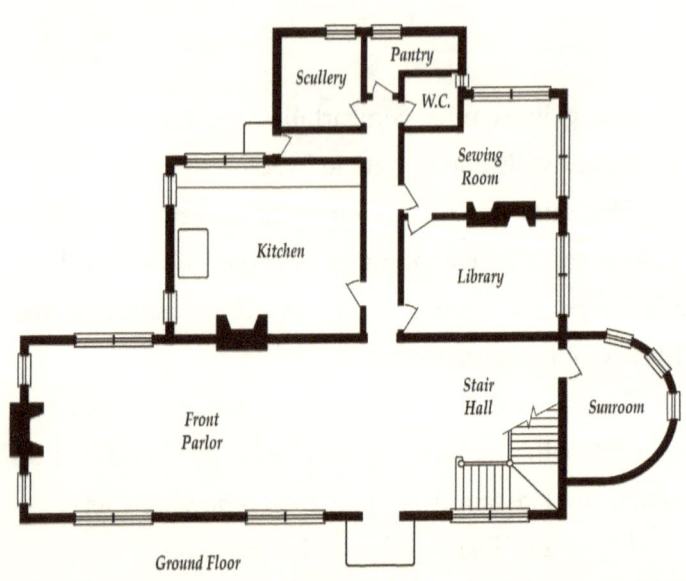

Scullery

Pantry

W.C.

Sewing
Room

Kitchen

Library

Front
Parlor

Stair
Hall

Sunroom

Ground Floor

Family Tree of the Calcinides

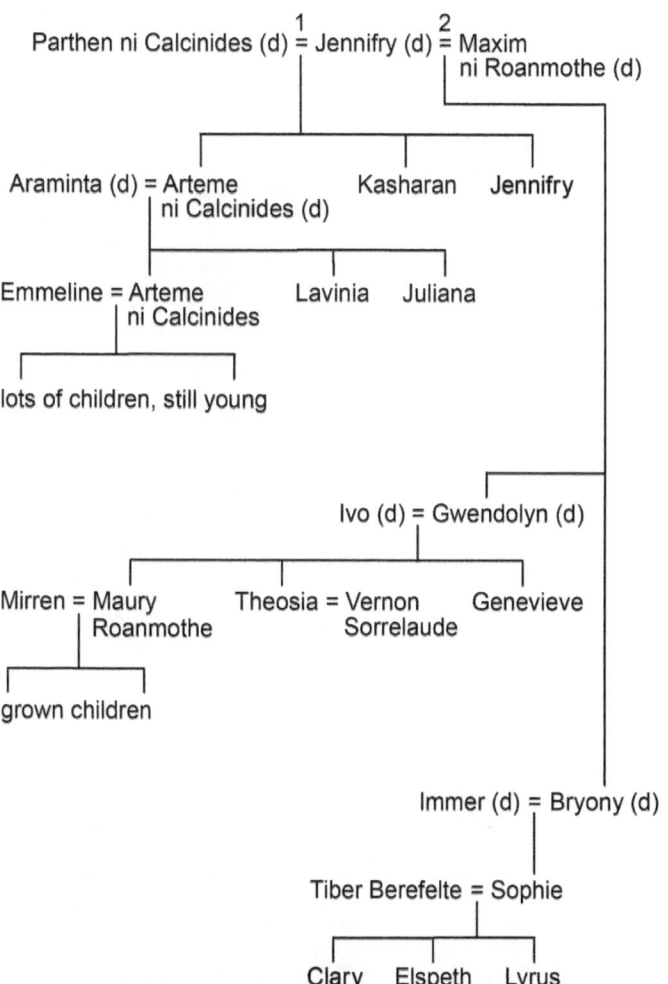

Justice in Auberon

Jennifry's nephew, Arteme ni Calcinides, serves as Justicar of the Peace for his *lething*. (A *lething* is a subdivision of a *worthing*. A *worthing* is similar to a county. Auberon possesses eighteen *worthings*.)

Being Justicar means Arteme presides over his Court Justicarate when issues such as petty theft, disorderly conduct, or trespass arise. And dispenses summary justice, without formality, for smaller offenses: wearing inappropriate bathing costume, grazing your cow on your neighbor's land, moving a road sign, and the like.

Arteme passes no judgment on more serious crimes. Burglary, arson, and assault and battery all get referred to the next higher court, the Quintary Sessions, held five times a year and presided over by three Lord Justicars.

The worst breaches go higher still.

Murder and kidnapping must be tried at the Courts of Assidere, convened as necessary.

And treason goes all the way to the Morofane's Bench.

The structure of Auberon's judicial courts looks like this:

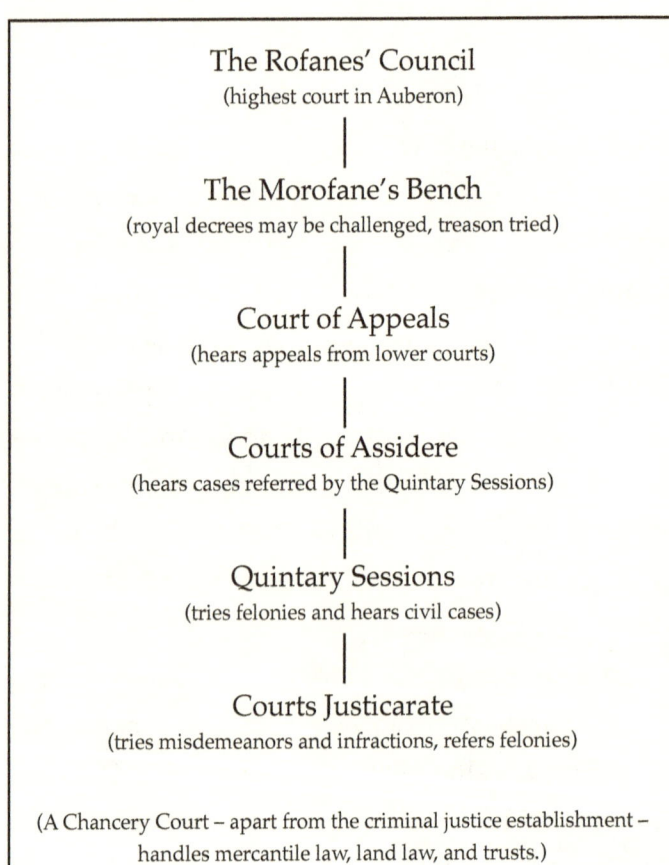

The Rofanes' Council
(highest court in Auberon)

The Morofane's Bench
(royal decrees may be challenged, treason tried)

Court of Appeals
(hears appeals from lower courts)

Courts of Assidere
(hears cases referred by the Quintary Sessions)

Quintary Sessions
(tries felonies and hears civil cases)

Courts Justicarate
(tries misdemeanors and infractions, refers felonies)

(A Chancery Court – apart from the criminal justice establishment –
handles mercantile law, land law, and trusts.)

Thus, when Clary and her family arrive at Arteme's manor house, reporting the violent death of Arteme's aunt – Kasharan – the Rofane must go investigate.

If the events prove to be death by misadventure, the case need go no further. But if murder is suspected, Arteme must refer the case to the Quintary Sessions along with a suspect and all the evidence pointing to that suspect. The Rofane has quite a job cut out for him!

Luckily, he has help.

In the distant past, his help would have consisted of the knights under his rule and their squires. But in these "modern" times, the Royal Judiciary appoints and funds a secretary – to handle records – as well as twenty stave-men – to make arrests – and five warders – to supervise the stave-men and handle especially challenging criminal situations.

However, these twenty-five men on active duty must secure the entire *lething*. As Arteme departs to investigate the scene of Kasharan's death, he has only four of them at hand.

Sophie's Bramble Conserve

four cups of bramble berries
two tea spoons of the salt of the sea
one-quarter cup of sugar
one-quarter cup of liquid whey
drained from curdled raw milk
2 tea spoons of dried apple pomace
2 tea spoons of well water

Wash the berries and drain them well. Place the berries in a bowl with all of the other ingredients. Mash the berries with a wooden mallet until they are thoroughly crushed. Stir the admixture well. Place the admixture into a scrupulously clean glass or crockery receptacle and seal it tightly. In summer, hold for two days on a pantry shelf. In winter, hold on the mantle above the bread ovens. After two to four days have passed, cool and serve. For lengthy storage, place in the ice house, and the conserve will stay good for two months.

Months of the Year

Janary winter

Falnary late winter

Nerich early spring

Thyril spring

Ponce late spring

Joiesse early summer

Labra summer

Jube late summer

Sanember early autumn

Ionaber autumn

Noulember late autumn

Bricember early winter

Days of the Week

Esstey Essey's Day, the Holy Day

Lundy Moon's Day

Teysdy Teyo's Day, God's Day

Wandy The Wanderer's Day

Barrsdy Barris' Day, Day of Strength

Fanishday Lady's Day

Beldy Beldaine's Day, Day of Gifts

Magic in the North-lands

Safe Magic

Civilized people in the North-lands use a gentle energy magic that is practical, but not flamboyant. It requires study and practice to achieve real skill.

Auberon's practitioners are called patterners or pattern-masters. Most are content to incline sick people toward health, to nudge crops into lush growth, and to adjust the worst storms into heavy downpours.

It's rare to heal someone near death, to grow fruit trees in non-arable land, or to disperse a hurricane. Even among the elite, such unusual feats are possible only if the underlying structures (the radices and the arcs) permit small repairs or adjustments to achieve spectacular results.

Practitioners merely help the natural processes along in a favorable direction. They do not change the energy configuration significantly. That would be *incantatio* or troll-magic, which is both dangerous and illegal.

Practitioners avoid large alterations to energy patterns. It's perilously easy to drift across the line separating the safe from the forbidden, when too much is attempted.

Perilous Magic

Troll-magic, or *incantatio*, is flamboyant, acute, and immediate in its effects. A troll-mage might pull a sick person back from the brink of death, grow watermelons in the desert, disperse a typhoon, or other such magnificent feats.

Unfortunately, it is the practice of troll-magic that turns humans into trolls.

It corrupts their bodies, starting with the ears and nose, which enlarge a little with each use of the power. It also unbalances their intellectual and emotional abilities.

A troll-witch who has practiced troll-magic for years will have a nose elongated like a curled thumb, ears the size of normal hands, swollen hands and feet, a severely curved spine, and much ill health. In his or her mind, insanity reigns.

Troll-magic is forbidden in all civilized places, because its use essentially creates powerful villains. A few intellectual types use the terms *incantatio* and incantor or incantress. But most folk call this perilous practice troll-magic and its practitioners troll-mages or troll-witches. Nobody really wants to separate the idea of the magic from its effect: making trolls.

Insane trolls do crazy and hurtful things with their power. Newer trolls usually flock to older and more powerful trolls in the wild lands. They have no place in the civilized world. The authorities arrest them, because they cannot be left at large, and sentence them to death. (Incarceration is impractical. How do you imprison someone who can break any cell?)

Trolls don't live long, because the troll-disease, once started, progresses. When it progresses too far, the troll dies. Even potent trolls who elude capture live short lives.

Auberon occupies the northern tip of the penninsula just above Cambers and Solmondy. The island nations of Fiorish and Erice lie north and northeast of Auberon. The Merovessic Sea stretches to its west.

Timeline for the North-lands Stories

ANCIENT TIMES

Skies of Navarys..........3000 years before *Perilous Chance*

THE BRONZE AGE

Resonant Bronze ....2000 years before *Perilous Chance*

BEFORE THE STEAM AGE

Rainbow's Lodestone.. ~100 years before *Perilous Chance*

Star-drake........... immediately after *Rainbow's Lodestone*

THE STEAM AGE

Sarvet's Wanderyar ....52 years before *Perilous Chance*

Crossing the Naiad ... concurrent with *Sarvet's Wanderyar*

Livli's Gift ....38 years after *Sarvet's Wanderyar*
(14 years before *Perilous Chance*)

Troll-magic .... contemporaneous with *Perilous Chance*

The Troll's Belt .. contemporaneous with *Perilous Chance*

Perilous Chance ....the now of this timeline

J.M. Ney-Grimm lives with her husband and children in Virginia, just east of the Blue Ridge Mountains. She's learning about permaculture gardening and debunking popular myths about food. The rest of the time she reads Robin McKinley, Diana Wynne Jones, and Lois McMaster Bujold, plays boardgames like Settlers of Catan, *rears her twins, and writes stories set in her troll-infested North-lands.*

Look for her novels and novellas at your favorite bookstore – online or on Main Street.

J.M. Ney-Grimm maintains a blog featuring flash fiction from her North-lands and other tidbits unearthed by her ever-active curiosity.

Visit her at http://JMNey-Grimm.com.